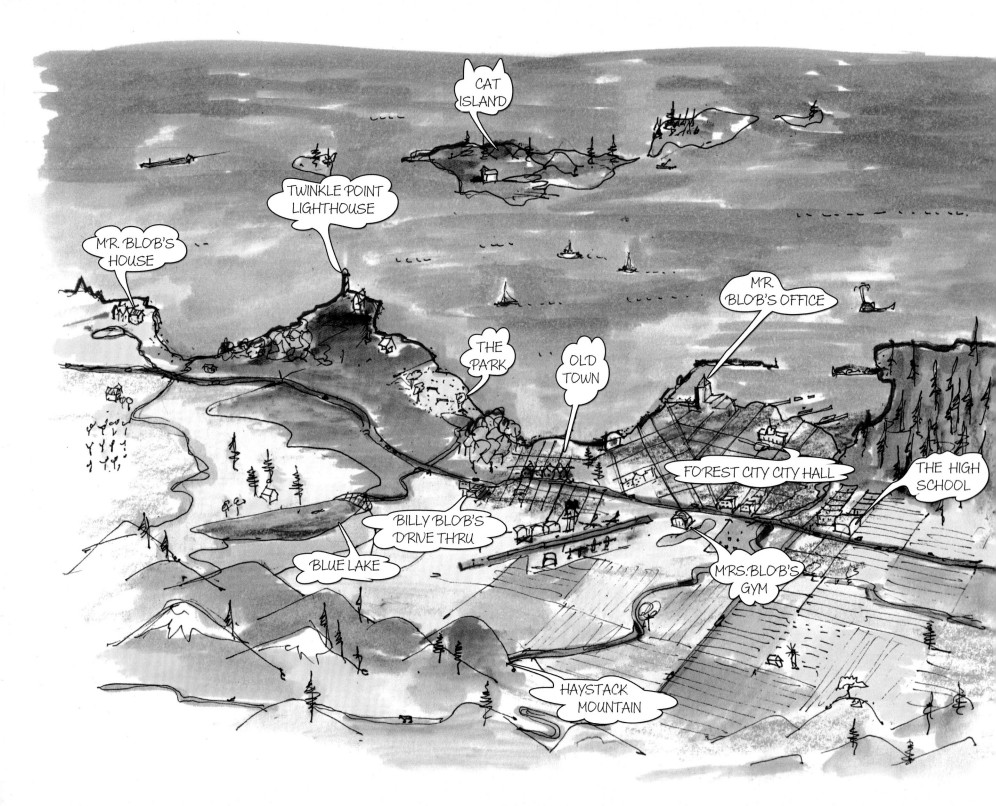

JULIE GORDON
AUTHOR

This Book Is Dedicated
By Julie With Love
To Audrey and Charlie
and
By Michael to His Mom
Gloria Fay Murphy

MICHAEL KENT MURPHY
ILLUSTRATOR

ISBN 978-0-615 33260-4

First Edition, 2009
Printed in the U.S.A.
by Auburn Printers and Integrated Marketing
www.auburnprinters.com

Published by Gordon And Murphy Publishing
P.O.Box 580, Applegate CA. 95703
www.misterblob.com

MR. BLOB LOSES HIS JOB

AND LEARNS SOMETHING WONDERFUL

Mr. Blob LOVES his family. They live in a beautiful Mansion.
They have shiny new cars, boats and bicycles. Mr. Blob has a FABULOUS
staff that takes care of his home so his family has time to do whatever makes them happy.

Mr. Blob works all the time
but he is proud of the things he can provide
for his family. There is NOTHING he won't do to keep his family happy.

Mr. and Mrs. Blob leave their house
early in the morning, just as the sun is rising.
They drive to the country club so Mrs. Blob can have
her daily beauty treatment. "I think I will get the banana cream facial
today. I want to look nice for our dinner tonight. See you after work," says Mrs. Blob.

Billy Blob stops
for breakfast on his way
to school. "I'll have hash browns,
one soft taco, two hot dogs and a large chocolate shake," he says.

Brittney and Brandy Blob
have their usual breakfast of doughnuts
and sodas. "You need to wipe the chocolate off your mouth
and grab your books. I don't want to miss the bus again!" Brittney tells Brandy.

The house is quiet
and the Blobs' pets, Bernie,
Buffy and Binky, realize no one remembered to feed them, AGAIN!

After work
Mr. & Mrs. Blob dine
on steaks and fries with a
chocolate sundae for dessert.
They drive home after their meal
and find the house dark and the kitchen
counter piled high with empty pizza boxes and soda cans.

Mr. Blob arrives
at work early Monday morning.
There is a note on his desk to see
the boss as soon as he gets in. "Bob old boy,
I'm afraid I have some BAD news," His boss says.
"It looks like we've run out of money and I'll have to let you go."
He hands Mr. Blob his final paycheck and closes the door behind him.

Mr. Blob worries
as he drives home. "What
will I say to my family? How
will I tell them I lost my job? What
will happen when I can't make the payments
on our house? Our lives will never be the same!!!"

The Blobs sit down
to dinner. Little Brandy thinks
it is a holiday because they NEVER have
family dinners. Mr. Blob tells them that he has
lost his job. They all think of what this will mean to them.

Mr. Blob
starts looking
for a new job the very next day.

Mr. Blob pulls up
to the house that evening
after a long day of looking for work.
He can't help but smile when he sees his
daughter Brandy. "Look Daddy, I'm a hard worker
just like you!" Brandy says from her lemonade stand.
"I've already made fourteen dollars and twenty five cents!"

When he walks
around the back of
the house he sees Brittney
hanging out the laundry. "I can
save us money by doing more of the housework.
Now we won't need a maid!" Britney proudly announces.

Just then,
Billy rides up
the driveway on his
bike. "Hey Dad," Billy yells
out of breath. "I got a job
delivering newspapers and it pays
twenty dollars a week, plus tips!" Mr.
Blob can't believe how much the kids are helping out!

Mr. Blob
rounds up the kids
and they head inside. As
they walk into the kitchen the
smell of freshly baked bread makes their
stomachs rumble. Mrs. Blob has prepared a wonderful
home-cooked meal. "It's a lot cheaper to eat at home,"
She says."Besides, I forgot how much fun cooking can be!"

Grandma and Grandpa Blob
join the rest of the family for the wonderful meal.
"Wow," says Brandy. "I love family dinners!"They talk
and laugh about their busy day and how tired and happy they all feel.

Mr. Blob goes out every day
looking for work. One evening Grandpa
Blob calls. "Hey Son, Mr. Butts at the bike shop is retiring and
I just saw a "help wanted" sign in his window!" Mr. Blob applies for the job and lands it!

The next week,
Grandma Blob sees a "FOR SALE"
sign on the little house down the street
from them. Grandpa calls his son with the good news.
"You won't believe the price on the house down the street
from us! It's a STEAL. All it needs is a LITTLE fixing up," Grandpa says.

The Blob family gathers all their money and
puts a down payment on the little house. Everyone
works hard to fix up their new home. Grandpa fixes
the fence and front porch. Grandma cleans all of the
windows. Brittney and Brandy do all the painting. Mr. Blob
and Billy Blob repair the roof and chimney. Mrs. Blob helps
lay the mortar. They work hard and laugh a lot and make the little house a home.

The next day
the family packs up
everything that will fit in their
new little house. They sell their cars
and boat and all of their fancy furniture.
They pack up what is left and drive across town to their new home and their new life.

Mr. Blob grills up
the burgers on a sunny day.
He thinks about how lucky he was to lose that job
and find what happiness really is. Not cars and boats,
but family and friends and the TIME to enjoy them all!

THE END

HOW CAN YOU HELP YOUR FAMILY?

LOOK FOR UPCOMING BOOKS
ABOUT THE BLOB FAMILY

Mr. Blob Goes Green

The Blobs Take a Vacation

Mr.Blob's Farmers Market

contact@misterblob.com